caillou®

The Captain

Adaptation of the animated series: Sarah Margaret Johanson
Illustrations: CINAR Animation; adapted by Eric Sévigny

chouette   COOKIE JAR

Today Caillou and Grandpa were going to the park. Grandpa arrived at Caillou's house carrying a box. "What's in the box, Grandpa?" Caillou asked. "You'll see when we get to the park," Grandpa replied.

Caillou was so curious to know what was in the box.
On the bus ride to the park, Caillou played a guessing
game with Grandpa in order to find out.
"Is it a soccer ball? Or a kite? I know, it's a helicopter!"
"No, no, no," replied Grandpa.

"Grandpa, look at all the boats!" Caillou shouted.
He loved to watch the boats on the pond.
"They're having a race! I wish we had a... Oh, wow!
A sailboat!"
"I made it myself. Do you like it?" Grandpa asked,
as he pulled a sailboat out of the box.
"Oh, yes! Does it really sail?"

Soon they had the boat in the water. Caillou was very excited when Grandpa let him do the steering! "I'm steering it!" Caillou exclaimed.

"That's right! Captain Caillou. Just be careful. If you turn it too fast, it'll tip over," Grandpa said.

"Can we race with the other boats, Grandpa?" Caillou asked.

"Let's get lined up for the start," Grandpa said.
"Hi, Caillou," said Emma, Caillou's friend from playschool.
"Hi, Emma," Caillou replied. "Are you going to race, too?"
"Yes, my boat is the red one. And that boy over there has the blue boat."

"I bet we win, Grandpa!" Caillou said, confidently.
"Maybe we will," Grandpa replied. "But remember that the most important thing is to have fun. The finish line is the other side of the pond. On your mark, get set, GO!"

"My boat is faster than your boat!" Caillou shouted. "No, it isn't! Come on!" Emma replied, encouraging her boat.
Caillou really wanted to win, so he made his boat go a little faster.

"Be careful, Caillou," Grandpa warned. "Not too fast."
"We're winning! Faster, faster!" Caillou shouted. "Oh, no!"
Caillou's boat ran into Emma's, and both boats tipped over.
"That's too bad, Caillou. Better luck next time," Grandpa said.

Caillou felt bad because he had lost
and he had made Emma lose, too.
"Sorry, Emma," Caillou said, shyly.
"Oh, that's all right. I come here with
my Daddy every weekend, and my
boat always tips over."

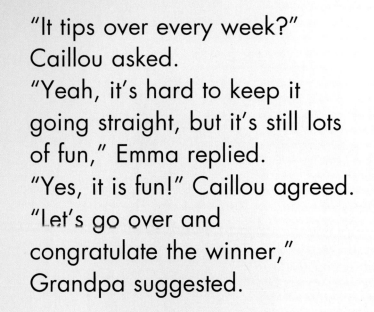

"It tips over every week?"
Caillou asked.
"Yeah, it's hard to keep it
going straight, but it's still lots
of fun," Emma replied.
"Yes, it is fun!" Caillou agreed.
"Let's go over and
congratulate the winner,"
Grandpa suggested.

On the way home, Grandpa asked Caillou, "Are you disappointed that you didn't win the race?"
"I was a little," Caillou replied. "But I liked being Captain Caillou, even if I didn't win!"

Text adapted by Sarah Margaret Johanson from the scenario of the CAILLOU animated film series produced by Cookie Jar Entertainment Inc. (©1997 CINAR Productions (2004) Inc., a subsidiary of Cookie Jar Entertainment Inc.).
All rights reserved.
Original story written by Thor Bishopric and Todd Swift
Original episode: "Captain Caillou" #313
Illustrations taken from the television series CAILLOU and adapted by Eric Sévigny.
Art Direction: Monique Dupras

Bibliothèque et Archives nationales du Québec and Library and Archives Canada cataloguing in publication

Johanson, Sarah Margaret, 1968-
Caillou: the captain
(Clubhouse)
For children aged 3 and up.

ISBN 978-2-89450-747-6

1. Pleasure - Juvenile literature. I. . Sévigny, Éric. II. Title. III. Title: Captain. IV. Series: Clubhouse.

BF515.J63 2010   j152.4'2   C2009-941988-2

Legal deposit: 2010

We gratefully acknowledge the financial support of BPIDP and SODEC for our publishing activities.

Printed in China
10 9 8 7 6 5 4 3 2 1   6595013